TOUCHDOWN TROUBLE

FRED BOWEN series
SPORTS STORY

TOUCHDOWN TROUBLE

FRED BOWEN

PEACHTREE
ATLANTA

Published by
PEACHTREE PUBLISHERS
1700 Chattahoochee Avenue
Atlanta, Georgia 30318-2112
www.peachtree-online.com

Cover design by Thomas Gonzalez and Maureen Withee.
Book design by Melanie McMahon Ives

Printed and bound in the United States of America
10 9 8 7 6 5 4 3 2 1
First Edition

Library of Congress Cataloging-in-Publication Data
Bowen, Fred.
      Touchdown trouble / written by Fred Bowen.
         p. cm.
      Summary: Sam is proud that his touchdown in the final play of a game left his football team undefeated, but when a video-recording of the game reveals that the touchdown was scored illegally, he and the other Cowboys must decide whether to reveal the truth. Includes facts about a similar situation faced by Cornell University's team after a game with Dartmouth in 1940.
      ISBN 13: 978-1-56145-497-6 / ISBN 10: 1-56145-497-4
      [1. Football--Fiction. 2. Honesty--Fiction. 3. Sportsmanship--Fiction.] I. Title.
      PZ7.B6724Tou 2009
      [Fic]--dc22
                            2008054867

To the memory of Eric Ehrenberg—

colleague, sports fan, and a Cornell man

through and through

S am Danza reached above his desk and grabbed his favorite book from the shelf. He flopped down on his bed, turned on his side, and propped himself up on one elbow. For a few seconds, he just smiled and stared down at the book. It was a red three-ring binder. The cover read: *Cowboys Playbook.*

Sam was twelve years old and the star running back for the Cowboys in the Woodside Football League. He loved studying his playbook.

Sam leaned over to turn on the lamp next to his bed and opened the book. The first page had a diagram of his favorite play, the I-34.

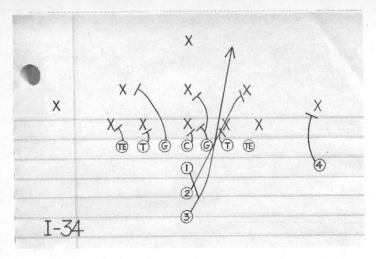

I-34

Lying back in his Cowboys shirt, Sam closed his eyes and imagined himself lining up behind Eddie Ching, his friend and the team's fullback. He saw Trey Johnson, the Cowboys quarterback, get the hike, turn, and slip the ball to him. With his eyes still closed, Sam imagined himself running with the football. He could feel the tacklers grabbing for his legs and feet as he pulled away, still running. He could hear the crunch of the players against each other. He could even smell the grass, sweat, and dirt.

Sam sat up and flipped through the pages to another play, the I-38. In that play

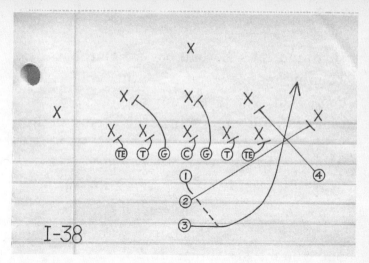

I-38

Sam took the handoff and ran around the right end. Sam closed his eyes again and lay back on his pillow. He imagined Trey calling out the signals.

"Ready...set..."

Again he saw the Cowboys linemen getting into their three-point football stances in time with the signals. He felt the whole team ready to surge forward the moment Trey yelled *"Hut!"*

Just then Sam's father knocked on the door and poked his head into the room. "What are you doing, Sam?"

"Huh?" Sam said, his eyes popping open. He was surprised to find himself in his bed, surrounded by football posters on the walls. Then he realized that his father was at the door. "Oh, I'm just studying the plays for tomorrow's game against the Steelers," he said.

"You already know those plays pretty well," Mr. Danza said. "You've played four games and you guys haven't lost yet."

"Yeah, I guess. But I don't want to be the one who messes things up."

"Well, okay, but turn off your light soon," Mr. Danza said. "You know your mom doesn't like you staying up late when you're with me."

Sam nodded. His parents were divorced, and he spent every Friday night during the football season at his dad's house. "I'll go to sleep in a little while," he said. "I need to go over a few more plays."

"Okay. See you in the morning." Sam's father closed the door behind him.

Sam looked back at the binder and turned the page. His dad was right. Sam knew every play by heart. But he loved reliving the plays and games as he lay in the quiet darkness of his room, lit only by his small bedside lamp. He closed his eyes again and saw himself running with the football, leaving the tacklers in the dust. He heard the crowd cheering as he sprinted down the field.

Sam loved football. He loved being the Cowboys' best running back, the guy everyone counted on to carry the ball and score touchdowns. But most of all, he loved that feeling he got when the Cowboys were all working together—when they were pushing the other team back, gaining yardage on every play, and getting closer and closer to the end zone.

He closed the playbook and thought about the next day's game. That was what he loved most about football: knowing that the Cowboys were really a team.

Chapter 2

I-34 on two. Break!" The Cowboys clapped their hands in perfect unison and turned to line up against the Steelers. Sam stood with his hands on his knees in the backfield behind Eddie. His friend was shorter and wider than Sam, making him the perfect blocker. Sam tried not to look at the space between the Cowboys right guard and right tackle. I-34 meant that he would take the handoff and run hard toward that spot.

Trey, the Cowboys quarterback, walked confidently up to the line of scrimmage, crouched behind the center, and barked out signals. "Ready…set…hut…hut."

On the second count, the Cowboys line

surged forward. Trey spun around, clutching the football close to his chest. Eddie ran by him and blasted into the Steelers line, trying to clear a path for Sam. Trey slipped the ball against Sam's stomach. Sam held it tight and quickly checked the position of the Cowboys right guard and tackle. There was no opening, just a tangle of Cowboys and Steelers.

Sam dug his left foot in the turf and darted farther to the right. A Steelers linebacker rushed forward. Sam spun left. The linebacker reached for Sam, but only got a piece of his leg. Sam shook him off and shot downfield. He was gaining ground, moving fast, when, *crunch!*—a wall of Steelers tacklers stopped him and sent him crashing into dirt.

Mr. Johnson, Trey's dad and the coach for the Cowboys, paced the sidelines and cheered on the team. "Good run, Sam!" he shouted. "That's the way to go for the extra yards. Keep it going, Cowboys."

The referee took the ball from Sam and walked to the middle of the field. He placed the ball on the ground and pointed down the field. "First down!" he called.

Walking back to the Cowboys huddle, Sam looked up into the stands. In the top row, Sam's father stood behind a compact digital camcorder on a tripod. He looked out from behind the camera and gave Sam a thumbs-up signal. His father filmed all the Cowboy games.

Back in the huddle, Trey was all business. "Nice run. Let's keep it going. Fake I-33, square-in pass, right on one."

This time Trey faked the handoff, slipping the ball away from Sam at the last second, and faded back to pass. Sam folded his arms around his stomach to make the Steelers think he had the ball and crashed into the line.

Wham! Sam hit the ground hard, smacked down by a Steelers tackler. But when he heard the cheers he knew the fake had worked. He looked up and saw Jared Sims, the Cowboys wide receiver, on the ground with the ball about fifteen yards downfield.

"First down!" the referee called again.

The Cowboys sideline burst into cheers.

"Good catch, Jared!"

"Great throw, Trey!"

"Way to go, line!"

Trey kept calling plays and the Cowboys kept moving the ball down the field. Finally the Cowboys had the ball on the Steelers eight-yard line. First down, eight yards to go for a touchdown. Sam looked past the Cowboys huddle to the Steelers defense. The Steelers linemen had their hands on their hips and were breathing hard.

Back in the Cowboys huddle, Manny DeCastro, their best lineman, spoke up. "Let's run it right at them," he said. "They're done."

"Yeah, come on, Trey," Eddie said. "Right up the gut. We'll score on the first play."

Trey scanned the Steelers huddle. Sam followed his eyes and noticed a lineman trying to rest. He was down on one knee with his helmet off. *Good*, he thought. *They're getting tired.*

"Okay," Trey said. "Sam's gonna go right up the middle. I-32 on one."

On Trey's command, the Cowboys line blasted forward. This time Sam needed no fancy footwork. He took off as fast as he could, leaving the Steelers way behind. He raced into the end zone and raised his arms in triumph.

Touchdown!

The Cowboys added a two-point conversion, and Sam looked up at the scoreboard as the team trotted off the field.

The Cowboys were ahead 22–6 with only five minutes to play.

Coach Johnson pumped his fist as the players returned to the sidelines. "Way to mix it up, Trey! Great blocking—Sam could have *walked* in. Come on, let's play defense! We've got this game!"

The Cowboys played hard and held on to win 22–6.

After the game the tired players walked slowly off the field with their helmets at their sides. Their faces were red from playing hard and their jerseys were soaked with sweat. They all gulped water as fast as they could.

"Hey, are you guys still undefeated?" Brady Hall, the quarterback for the Giants, called out as he waited on the sideline for the next game.

The Giants were the Cowboys' biggest rivals and Brady was their best player. The two teams were scheduled to play each other the next Saturday.

"Yeah," Sam called back. "We're 5 and 0."

"Well, you won't be undefeated for long. We'll see *you* later," Brady said, pointing at the Cowboys. He put on his helmet and walked toward the field with a group of his teammates.

"Sounds like he thinks he knows who's gonna win next Saturday," Eddie said as he watched Brady walk away.

"The Giants are pretty good," Sam said. "And so's Brady."

"Maybe," Trey said.

Sam's father came down onto the field, carrying the camera and smiling from ear to ear. "Great game," he said, slapping Sam on his shoulder pads. "You must have had more than a hundred yards rushing."

"Thanks to my great blocking," Eddie said, tapping his chest with his thumb.

"Yeah, you looked good, too." Mr. Danza patted his camera. "You should all have fun watching this game at our house Friday."

Sam squirted some cool water from his bottle against his forehead. "Yeah, it'll get us pumped for the game Saturday."

Sam's father looked across the field to where the Giants were doing their warm-up drills in a big circle. "Do you want to watch the Giants play for a while?" he asked.

Sam shook his head, sending sweat and water flying like he was a wet dog shaking itself dry. "Nah," he said. "We'll get to see them soon enough."

"Fake I-21, swing pass, right on one." Sam lined up in back of Eddie. His hands rested on his bare knees with his wrists touching the edge of his blue mesh basketball shorts.

"Ready...set...hut."

Trey spun around, faked a handoff to Eddie, and glided back to throw.

Sam darted to the right and powered up the field. Jared, the wide receiver, cut left, leaving the right side clear for Sam.

Trey looked to the right and tossed a perfect spiral. Sam caught it in full stride and ran up the empty field, faking out tacklers who weren't there. Finally he turned and trotted back to his three teammates.

"Nice throw," he said as he flipped a pass to Trey. "I didn't have to slow down at all for that one."

"See, the fake I-21's a great play," Trey said, pointing with the football as he spoke to his teammates. "It lets us get the ball to Sam in the open downfield. There's no way anyone will stop him."

"Yeah," Eddie agreed. "Sam's got good hands and he can get by the linebacker."

Trey spun the football in his hands. "We're gonna need to run the ball less and pass more against the Giants. They've got some big dudes in the middle of the line," he said.

Sam smiled. Trey talked and thought just like a coach. Maybe that was because his father, Coach Johnson, *was* the coach.

"Let's run it again," Trey said, slapping the side of the football.

Sam ran his hand through his sweaty hair to get it away from his eyes. It was October, but it was still shorts weather.

"On two. Ready…set…hut…hut."

Once again Sam ran right and then swung upfield. Trey gave him a pump fake and floated the ball long. Sam reached out, caught the ball on his fingertips, and sprinted up the field and into the end zone. He raised both hands—one still gripping the ball—high above his head to signal a touchdown.

"That's a pretty good play," a voice called. "Want to run it against a real defense?"

Sam glanced at the sideline and saw Brady Hall and three more members of the Giants standing at the edge of the field. Brady held a football on his hip and the others had their arms folded across their chests.

Eddie jogged up beside Sam. "Look who's here," he whispered.

"Yeah, just what we need," Sam said under his breath.

"The play won't work if you guys know it's coming," Trey called out.

"Yeah, okay," Brady said as the Giants moved across the field and closer to the Cowboys. He was a step ahead of his teammates and a lot taller. "You guys want to play a game of touch football?"

Sam thought Brady's words sounded more like a challenge than a question.

"Sure," Sam said. "What are the teams?"

"What do you think?" Brady said, holding his hand out to the side to gather in his teammates. "Giants against the Cowboys. Just like it'll be on Saturday."

"Okay," Trey agreed. "You guys kick off."

"Why us?" one of the Giants asked.

"Because you picked the teams," Trey said as he and the other Cowboys headed toward one side of the field.

Trey and Sam shouted out the rules of the game as they walked backwards to their side.

"Two-hand touch, no tackle."

"You gotta count to three Mississippi before you can rush the quarterback."

"Four downs to score a touchdown."

"Three straight complete passes gives the offense a first down."

"But they've got to be real passes," Brady protested. "No wimpy one-yard tosses."

The game started rough and got rougher with every play. Some of the two-hand touches were as tough as any tackle. The Cowboys scored first on a short pass from Trey to Eddie, but the Giants grabbed the lead with two scores.

"Man, Brady is good," Sam whispered to Trey as they walked back to receive the kickoff. "He can really throw the ball."

"He's not so hot," Trey muttered. "We'll come back."

Sure enough, the Cowboys knotted the score at two touchdowns when Trey lofted a perfect spiral to Sam for a long score.

When the Cowboys got the ball back after stopping the Giants a few plays later, Trey looked around. The field was growing dark. Streetlights were on and car headlights twinkled in the distance. "Next touchdown wins, okay?" he said.

"You're only saying that because you've got the ball," a Giant pointed out.

"We can't play in the dark," Sam said.

"Stop talking and play, will you?" Brady said.

The Cowboys gathered in a tight huddle. Trey drew a play with his finger on Jared's shirt as he told his teammates the plan. "Jared, you hike the ball. Eddie, you're the left end. Sam, you're on the right. Both of you go down about five yards and cross." Trey's fingers crossed on Jared's shirt. Then he pointed to Eddie. "Don't worry about getting open," he said. "But make sure you get in the way of the guy covering Sam. Don't block him, just give him a nudge."

Sam looked over to the Giants. "That's an illegal pick," he said. "They might call offensive pass interference."

"I don't see any refs out here," Trey said, shrugging. "I'll pass it to you when you get open."

Sam lined up at the right end, just as Trey had instructed. He ran down five yards and angled left toward the middle of the field. As planned, Eddie nudged the Giant covering Sam. Suddenly Sam was open.

Trey's throw sailed high and Sam leaped, stretching as tall as he could. The ball skimmed off his fingertips.

Wham! Brady shoved Sam with a hard, two-handed push to the chest.

Thud! Sam fell backward before his feet touched the ground. His head smacked hard against the dry, hard-packed dirt. He lay on the ground, blinking his eyes. He could hear angry voices all around him.

"What do you think you're doing?" Trey asked, charging at Brady.

"Playing football," the Giants quarter-back snapped.

"It's supposed to be *touch* football."

"So what? I'm allowed to keep a guy from catching a pass."

Sam pulled his head up and rested on his elbows. "I'm okay," he said. "Trey, I'm okay."

"You could have really hurt him!" Trey shouted at Brady. He pointed to Sam. "Look at him."

"He said he's okay," Brady said. "And come on, you're the guys running the illegal offensive interference plays."

"Sam! Sam...time to go."

Sam turned and saw his mother waving from the parking lot.

"I gotta go," Sam said, struggling to his feet.

"You want to keep playing?" Brady asked the other Cowboys.

"No way," Trey said, grabbing his football and heading toward the parking lot with Sam, Eddie, and Jared. Trey looked back over his shoulder to the field. "It's a tie game," he shouted. Then he muttered to Sam, "What a jerk!"

"He's not being a jerk. Brady just plays hard and he really hates to lose," Sam said. "Kind of like you, Trey," he added.

"Yeah, I guess," Trey agreed. "That's why it'll be so much fun to beat him on Saturday—in a real game!"

Chapter 4

The Cowboys gathered noisily around Coach Johnson, who quickly held up his clipboard for quiet. "Okay, good practice today, guys. I like the hustle. I like the concentration." He paused to make sure everyone was listening. "We're gonna need lots of that hustle and concentration against the Giants this Saturday."

Sam looked at Eddie and Trey. The boys nodded and gave each other quick fist taps. They could hardly wait to play the Giants, especially after the touch football game.

"Remember, the game is at two o'clock," Coach Johnson continued. "That means I want you there, ready to play, at one thirty. If you're there at one thirty-one, you're late."

Sam tried not to laugh. *Nobody is going to be late for this game*, he thought.

"I don't have to tell you guys how important this game is," Coach Johnson said, lowering his voice a bit. "The Giants are undefeated, 5–0, same as us. The winner of this game has a good chance of winning the league championship." The coach let the team think about that for a moment and then shouted, "Okay, hands in!"

The Cowboys pressed in close and piled their hands in the center of the circle.

"What are we going to do Saturday?" Coach Johnson shouted as he put his left hand on top of the pile.

"Beat the Giants!" the Cowboys yelled.

"I can't hear you," Coach Johnson said, cupping his right hand to his ear.

"Beat the Giants!"

"Louder!"

"BEAT THE GIANTS!"

"That's more like it," the coach said with a big smile. "See you Saturday."

The players picked up their jackets, water bottles, and backpacks and headed home. "Hey, Trey," Coach Johnson called to his son. "I've got to run some errands. You want to come with me and grab a sub later?"

"Nah, that's all right," Trey said, standing next to Sam and Eddie. "I'll walk home with these guys."

"Okay, I'll see you there," his dad said with a wave.

Eddie pulled his scooter off the ground.

"Don't you go anywhere without that thing?" Trey asked.

"I like it. It's better than walking," Eddie said. With one foot on the scooter and one foot on the sidewalk, he pushed forward alongside his buddies. "Plus it saves my legs for running."

"Maybe I should get one," Sam said. "I'm the runner. You're the blocker."

"Aren't you guys a little old for scooters?" Trey teased.

"No, scooters are cool," Eddie said as he sped up and popped a wheelie. Trey and Sam laughed as they ran to catch up with him.

"Man, I wish it were Saturday already," Sam said. "I want to play those Giants right now."

"Me too," Eddie said.

"Well, I don't want to play the Giants," Trey said. He looked very serious.

Sam stopped walking. "*What?*" he said.

Eddie stopped his scooter. "Are you crazy?" he asked.

"I want to *beat* the Giants," Trey said with a big grin.

The three boys started moving again. "They're gonna be tough, though," Sam said. "Brady is a really good quarterback."

"Better than me?" Trey asked, pretending to be mad.

"Okay, maybe not as good as you, but he's still good," Sam said. "Remember that touch football game?"

"Yeah, and the Giants crushed the Eagles 26–0. We only beat them 14–6," Eddie said.

"They were just running up the score because they're a bunch of jerks," Trey said with a wave of his hand. "We could have beaten the Eagles by more."

Sam stayed quiet. He wasn't so sure Trey was right. The Giants game would be the toughest game of the year—by far. He reached into the front pocket of his hooded sweatshirt. "You guys want gum?"

"Sure."

After handing out his last piece, Sam walked over to a big metal barrel at the far corner of the parking lot. As he threw away the empty package, he saw something shiny leaning against the trash barrel. "Hey, check this out," Sam called out to the boys across the parking lot.

"What's the deal?" Trey asked as he walked toward Sam.

"Someone threw away a scooter," Sam said. He pointed at the two-wheeler propped against the barrel.

"What do you mean?" Trey asked. "You think someone just left it here?"

"Yeah, that's a Razor A3," Eddie said, gliding up on his own scooter. "And it's in pretty good shape. Who'd throw that away?"

"What are you talking about?" Sam said.

"There's nobody around. It doesn't belong to anybody. Somebody had to have thrown it away."

Trey shrugged. "Maybe they just forgot it."

"Come on," Sam said. "I mean, look, it's in the trash."

"It's not *in* the trash," Trey said. "It's *beside* the trash."

"That's because it can't fit in the barrel," Sam said as he picked up the scooter.

"I don't know, Sam," Eddie said. "See if it works."

Sam lifted up the scooter to get a closer look. Then he gave it a test ride across the parking lot.

"Does it run okay?" Trey called out to Sam.

"I need to test the brakes," Sam called back. He pushed his heel down on the brake and the scooter jerked to a stop. "I think it sticks a little bit."

"Maybe that's why they threw it away," Eddie said.

"Yeah, probably," Sam said.

"You gonna keep it?" asked Trey.

"Why not?" said Sam. "I can fix it."

"Bad brakes. Gee, that could be dangerous!" Trey said in a teasing voice.

"Maybe for a little kid, but not for me," Sam said.

"So, you're going to keep it?" Trey asked again.

"I told you," Sam said. "Yes."

"Maybe somebody stole it and ditched it here," Eddie said.

But Sam wasn't listening. He stepped onto the scooter and pushed away, with Eddie and Trey following behind. As he picked up speed, Sam looked back and yelled, "Come on, Eddie. I'll race you!" Then he pushed the scooter even faster and sailed across the smooth parking lot. The early evening air felt cool against Sam's face. "You can't catch me, I'm the Scooter Man!" he sang out as he headed into the darkness.

Chapter 5

Okay, everyone, we need to set up our floor hockey teams. Count off by fours!" Mr. Hale, Woodside Middle School's physical education teacher, shouted as he marched down the long line of students. The kids in the Friday morning gym class obeyed. Mr. Hale was a no-nonsense man who was built like a pro football linebacker.

"One...two...three...four..."

The next group of four counted off: "One...two...three...four..."

After every student had called out a number, Mr. Hale said, "All the number ones, step forward. You're the A team."

Sam and Eddie slapped high fives after they stepped forward and realized they were on the same team.

"All the number twos, step forward."

Brady Hall and Marcus Phillips stepped forward.

"Hey look, the B team has Brady and that kid Marcus who plays halfback for the Giants," Sam whispered to Eddie. "They could be pretty tough."

"Maybe Brady can't play floor hockey," Eddie suggested.

"I bet he's good. I mean, he is the Giants quarterback." Sam looked at the other members of the A team as they received their plastic hockey sticks from Mr. Hale.

"At least we've got Kaylee Gillis," Sam said. "She's pretty good at sports."

"All right, people. We'll play two games of floor hockey. One on each side of the gym." Mr. Hale held up his hands for quiet as the four teams set up on the gym floor in front of their nets. He looked around the room. "Remember, absolutely no checking, no slap shots, no high sticks. Keep your sticks on the floor."

"Any goalies?" Sam asked, his voice echoing off the gym walls.

"No goalies," Mr. Hale answered. "I don't want to waste any time with kids putting on pads."

The game began and the gym filled with shouts and the sounds of plastic sticks slapping against plastic pucks and other sticks. The A team took the lead, 1–0, when Sam scored a goal with a strong wrist shot set up by a centering pass from Kaylee.

"Lucky goal," Brady said as Sam and Brady waited for the faceoff following the goal.

"We'll see," Sam said as the action began again.

Brady tied the score at 1–1 a minute later when he flicked the puck into the corner of the net.

"There's your answer," Sam said to Eddie as the A team regrouped after the goal. "Looks like Brady *can* play floor hockey."

"Five minutes!" Mr. Hale shouted above the clatter of sticks. "Then we'll switch teams."

The pace of the game picked up. Sam had the puck in the middle of the floor, but

Brady stole it, smashing his stick hard across Sam's ankles.

"Hey, watch it!" Sam yelled as Brady raced away.

Brady whipped a shot just inches wide of the net. Kaylee took control of the puck in the corner.

"Kaylee!" Sam shouted, slapping his plastic stick against the gym floor to get her attention. "I'm open."

Kaylee skimmed a pass across the smooth wood surface. Brady raced down the floor, following the puck. Sam stopped the puck with his stick and quickly turned toward the goal. But Brady, still moving fast, hip-checked Sam.

Sam hit the padding on the gym wall and fell. As Brady started to run away with the puck, Sam swung his stick wildly and managed to smack Brady's thigh.

Thwack!

Brady turned around, startled. "Watch the high stick!" he said.

"Watch the checking," Sam said, scrambling to his feet.

Brady's eyes were blazing as he charged Sam. "I barely touched you!" he shouted.

"Oh, come on!" Sam shouted back and tossed his stick at Brady's ankles.

Brady kept charging forward and threw his stick at Sam's feet. Sam braced himself for Brady's rush. Brady shoved Sam hard against the padded wall, and when Sam bounced off the wall he pushed Brady back even harder.

Tweeeet! Tweeeeeet! Tweeeeeeeet! A series of long, hard whistle shrieks cut through the noise in the gym.

Mr. Hale dashed across the gym and pulled the boys apart. "I don't want any of that in my gym!" he shouted.

Brady pointed at Sam. "He threw his stick at me," he said.

"He checked me into the wall," Sam said, pointing back at Brady.

"Quiet!" Mr. Hale shouted, holding the boys apart. "I want both of you down in Mr. Hanley's office...*now!*"

Minutes later Sam and Brady were sitting in two high-backed chairs in front of a large, cluttered desk. Mr. Hanley, the vice principal of Woodside Middle School, walked in. He was a big man who always seemed to be in a hurry. His tie hung loose around his neck, the top button on his white shirt was unbuttoned, and his sleeves were rolled up just below his elbows. Sitting down at his desk, he hit a few keys and checked his computer screen. "Okay, Mr. Danza and Mr. Hall," he said finally, leaning forward. "Neither of you boys is one of my regular customers. Would you mind telling me what this is all about?"

"We...uh...kind of got tangled up in gym," Brady said in a low voice.

Sam snuck a quick look at Brady. The boy's answer had surprised him. Sam figured Brady was going to blame him for everything, but he hadn't.

"It was a floor hockey game, Mr. Hanley," Sam added. "That's all."

"Well, Mr. Hale said you boys were fighting," Mr. Hanley said. He drummed his fingers on the desk as he studied Sam and Brady.

"We weren't fighting," Brady insisted.

"It was just hockey," Sam said.

"Yeah, I bumped into Sam and he hit me with his stick," Brady said. Then he added, "By accident."

"Mr. Hale *thought* we were fighting," Sam said.

"He said you threw your sticks at each other," Mr. Hanley said. "You pushed each other around. Are you saying Mr. Hale is making this stuff up?"

Sam and Brady said nothing. Sam looked down at the blue office rug.

"You know I can suspend you boys for fighting," Mr. Hanley said. He paused and added, "And that would mean that you couldn't play football this weekend."

Sam's heart pounded. Suspended? No football?

"That's the rule in the Woodside Football League," the vice principal said, looking sternly at the boys.

Sam and Brady glanced at each other and then back at Mr. Hanley.

"But I'm not going to suspend you this time," he said, "because I don't think I'll have any more trouble with you two." He stood up and cocked an eyebrow at Sam and Brady. "Will I?"

"No sir," Sam said.

"You don't have to worry about me, Mr. Hanley," Brady said. "Or Sam."

"Okay," Mr. Hanley said in a very serious tone. "Get back to class."

Sam and Brady stood up and moved quickly toward the door. As Sam turned the knob, Mr. Hanley called, "Save the rough stuff for tomorrow's game."

Chapter 6

The pizza man is here," Sam's father announced as he walked through the front door with four pizza boxes balanced in his hands.

The Cowboys cheered. "Peet-*za*…peet-*za*… peet-*za*," they chanted.

"Sam, you can get drinks for everybody," Mr. Danza said. "Eddie and Trey, help him out. Manny and Jared, would you grab the paper plates?"

They knew the routine as well as they knew their football plays. Every Friday night the team went to Sam's dad's house to watch film of the previous Saturday's game. No coaches. No other parents. And Mr. Danza always ordered pizza to eat while they watched the game film he had recorded from the stands.

The boys sprawled out on the floor and the two sofas in the big family room. Sam got out cups for all the guys and noticed that the team was sitting in certain groups like they always did. The linemen and the backs sat together, while the reserves sat scattered along the edge of the room.

"Have some veggies along with your pizza," Mr. Danza said as he placed a large plate of cut carrots, celery, and broccoli on the coffee table in the middle of the room. "Remember, to play like an athlete, you have to eat like an athlete." The players nodded. But the pizza disappeared a lot faster than the vegetables.

The large flat-screen television on the wall lit up. The boys cheered as they watched the Cowboys—in their blue shirts, white pants, and white helmets with blue star decals— run onto the field. The players shouted out comments between bites of pizza and gulps of soda as the game flashed by.

"Man, what a move."

"Nice block, Manny."

"Ooooh! That's gotta hurt."

Trey pointed at the screen with a pizza slice in his hand. "Here's that I-34 play where Sam makes that sweet move to the outside," he said.

Sam edged forward on the sofa as he watched himself on the screen, dashing to the outside and down the field before he was tackled.

The Cowboys jumped up. "First down!" they shouted.

"You should have cut back earlier, Sam," Trey observed. "You could have picked up a few more yards."

"Maybe," Sam said. "It was still a pretty good run."

"Yeah, but you'll be even faster tomorrow against the Giants," Trey teased. "Now that you *found* that scooter and can save your legs for running."

Sam smiled, even though Trey had made it sound like he hadn't really found the scooter in the trash.

"So how do you like that thing, anyway?" Trey asked.

"It's cool," Sam said. "I use it all the time. It's great for going between my mom's house and my dad's."

Eddie laughed. "Sam's almost popping wheelies better than me."

Trey turned the conversation back to the game film as he pointed to the screen again. "Here comes the square-in pass," he said. Again the room broke into cheers as the ball thumped into Jared's chest for a 15-yard gain.

"Nice pass, dude."

"Sweet fake. Sam got killed on that play."

"Jared was wide open!" Trey stood up in the middle of the room and signaled a first down.

The Cowboys kept cheering as they watched themselves hustle down the field for another touchdown against the Steelers on the widescreen TV.

"Hey, Trey," Manny said as the video showed Sam galloping through a big gap in the Steelers defense for a touchdown. "Look at the holes on those plays. The line is doing all the work. You're just handing off the ball."

"Yeah, you guys are doing great…against the Steelers." Trey shrugged and took a swig of soda. "Let's see how you do against the Giants."

"They're tough," Sam agreed. "I don't know if I'm going to gain a hundred yards against those guys!"

"We can handle them," Manny said.

"Like you guys handled that pizza?" Eddie said, pointing at the empty boxes on the coffee table.

"Hey, I heard Mr. Hanley almost tossed you out of school for fighting with Brady," Trey said to Sam. "It's a good thing you didn't get thrown out. You would have missed tomorrow's game."

Sam frowned and signaled Trey to be quiet. "I don't want my dad to find that out, okay?" he said in a low voice.

Just then Mr. Danza walked back into the room. "I don't think Coach is going to want you guys to run the ball tomorrow," he said as the game film ended. "I bet he'll call more sweeps and passes."

"Like Fake I-21, swing pass right!" Trey shouted. He picked up a pillow from the sofa and tossed it to Sam, who grabbed it just before it hit a lamp.

"Hey, watch it," Mr. Danza said, and then pointed to the messy room. "Guys, let's pick all this stuff up now."

The Cowboys snapped into action, grabbing the cups, plates, and pizza boxes. Sam tossed the pillow back to Trey. "I hope Coach does calls the new I-21 play. I think it'll work," he said.

"Guess we'll have to find out tomorrow," Eddie said. "What time is the game again?"

"Two o'clock," Sam answered. Then he turned to the room and yelled, "So what are we going to do at two o'clock tomorrow?"

"Beat the Giants!" the team shouted.

"Louder."

"Beat the Giants!"

"I can't hear you," Sam said, cupping his hand to his ear.

"BEAT THE GIANTS!"

Sam flopped back on the sofa and took in the whole scene. All the guys. The smell of the pizza. The blue light of the TV screen.

The Giants don't stand a chance, he thought.

Chapter 7

Come on, we've got to stop them on this play," Manny pleaded in the Cowboys' defensive huddle. "We can't let them get another first down."

Sam looked up at the scoreboard.

HOME 12 | 03:30 QTR 4 | VISITOR 16

The Cowboys trailed the Giants 16–12 with only three and a half minutes left in the game.

This had been the toughest game of the year for both teams. Everyone was playing hard, but the Giants were ahead because they had scored the two-point conversions after each of their touchdowns. The Cowboys had fallen just inches short, twice.

Now it was third down for the Giants with three yards to go for a first down. If the Cowboys didn't stop them, the Giants would be able to run out most of the clock in their next set of downs. But if the Cowboys stopped them now, the Giants would be forced to punt. Then the Cowboys would have a chance to turn things around.

A large crowd ringed the football field. The aluminum stands along the sideline were filled. Sam's father stood at the top row filming, as usual. Heavy, dark clouds hung low over the field, but so far the rain had held off.

Brady brought the Giants to the line of scrimmage and looked over the Cowboys defense. "Ready...set..."

Standing at his safety position, Sam guessed the Giants would try to gain the crucial three yards by running to the left side of the line. He crept up closer to the line as Brady barked out the count. "Hut...hut."

At the snap, Sam sprinted to where he thought the runner and the ball would go. He guessed right. Sam and another Cowboy tackler slammed into the Giants runner, tackling him two yards short of the first down.

"Time out! Time out!" Coach Johnson shouted.

The coach gathered the Cowboys near the sideline. The noise and the cheers of the crowd swirled around them. "Listen up," Coach Johnson said, looking around and talking fast. "We're gonna get the ball back with about two and a half minutes to play. We've got to work fast. We only have one time-out left." Coach lifted one finger and then pointed to Trey. "Call two plays at a time. Everybody line up fast. We're running the two-minute drill just like we did in practice."

The helmets in the tight circle around the coach nodded. Sam could feel his heart racing. The Cowboys didn't have much time to score a touchdown.

Sam made a fair catch off the Giants punt. He was on the Cowboys 31-yard line and time was running out. Things started moving so fast that the game became a blur. Trey hit Jared with a quick pass for a 12-yard gain and a first down. The Cowboys quarterback tried to get the team to line up quickly as the referees scrambled to move the first down chain and down markers along the sideline. "Come on, come on, hurry up! Line up, line up!"

Sam caught a quick pitch and ran to the right. He cut inside for a few yards and then angled back to the sideline to get out of bounds and stop the clock. He made it, tumbling over the sideline after a five-yard gain.

The referee signaled time out and the Cowboys had a chance to catch their breath. It was second down, five yards to go with almost two minutes left.

Trey stepped into the huddle. "Fake I-21, swing pass right, and then straight I-21 on the next play. Everything's on one."

Sam was ready for Fake I-21. Just like in practice, Trey faked the handoff to Eddie as Sam swung out to the right. The seconds were ticking away as Trey faded back and tossed a perfect pass to Sam. With the ball tight to his chest, Sam slipped by a Giants tackler and charged full-speed ahead. He was covering ground fast when Brady slammed him down hard. But Sam had already ripped off a big gain to the Giants 32-yard line.

The clock was still running as the Cowboys lined up and the Giants and the referees tried to catch up. Trey shouted more orders. "Hurry up! Second play! Move...move...move!"

Eddie blasted up the middle and battled the Giants defensive line for a quick four yards.

"Time out! Time out!" Coach screamed, then called his team to the sideline.

"We have no time-outs left," he said, almost out of breath. "Let's try a sideline pass to Jared and then a quick I-21 again. We've got to make every play count."

The Cowboys hustled to their positions. Trey fired a long pass to Jared, who made a diving catch at the Giants 12-yard line.

"All right!" Sam shouted, leaping into the air and rushing down the field.

But Jared had been tackled in bounds, so the precious seconds kept clicking away. Now all the Cowboys were shouting.

"Move up. Move up."

"Come on."

"First down. Let's go!"

Eddie took a quick handoff, but was buried in a pile of Giants. The bodies untangled as the seconds kept ticking away. There was no time for a huddle now. Trey moved around, frantically shouting out the play numbers to his teammates as they lined up. "I-36...I-36...I-36...hut."

Trey handed the ball off to Sam, who dashed toward a hole in the right side of the line. A Giant tackler yanked Sam's right arm. The ball popped loose.

"Fumble!"

Suddenly players from both teams were flying toward the ball. Lying on the ground,

Sam saw the ball bounce off a diving player's forearm and back toward him. Sam reached out, pulled it to his chest, and held on tight. He breathed a sigh of relief as the referee untangled the pile.

"Cowboys ball," the referee signaled and quickly placed the ball on the seven-yard line.

The clock was still running as Trey tried to get the Cowboys organized.

"I-34...I-34...no huddle!" he shouted.

Sam glanced at the down marker on the sidelines and saw a big, red number 2.

Second down with less than a minute to go, he thought.

Sam took the handoff, tripped over a lineman's leg, and fell hard at the line of scrimmage. No gain. He scrambled to his feet as Trey called the signals for a slant pass. Sam looked at the scoreboard clock. Twenty seconds...nineteen...

"Hut."

Trey took two quick steps back and fired a bullet pass to Jared. The Cowboys wide receiver took one step and was met by

Brady, who delivered a bone-crunching tackle at the three-yard line.

The cheers and yelling around the field grew louder. The dark clouds loomed lower. The two teams seemed caught in a circle of sound.

Trey shouted the final play through cupped hands. "I-38...I-38...Ready..."

The crowd started to count down the final seconds.

"Five...four..."

"Set..."

"Three...two..."

"Hut."

Trey took the snap just in time, spun to his right, and pitched the ball back to Sam.

Knowing this was the final play, Sam bolted toward the yellow flag at the front corner of the end zone. He hurdled a Giant tackler, stumbled, and with his last step dove toward the flag, stretching the ball in front of him. Sam felt the flag against his right arm as he tumbled over in a tangle of tacklers.

He looked up and saw the referee standing on the sideline at the edge of the end zone. The referee's arms were stretched high above his head.

Touchdown! The Cowboys had won, 18–16!

In an instant Trey, Eddie, Manny, Jared, and all the other Cowboys were jumping up and down at the corner of the end zone, screaming at the top of their lungs. The crowd pushed in around them just as the dark clouds opened and swept the field in a swirl of rain and wind. Brady and the other Giants, stunned, stood as still as the goalposts as they watched the Cowboys celebrate.

At the center of the happy circle of Cowboys, Sam held the ball high above his head. Beside him, Trey yanked off his helmet. "I can't wait to see this game again on Friday night!" he shouted above the noise of the crowd.

Chapter 8

"Peet-*za*...peet-*za*...peet-*za*," the Cowboys chanted as Mr. Danza walked through the front door. The Cowboys were even more pumped up than usual for their Friday night film session. They all wanted to see the big 18–16 victory over the Giants.

"Settle down, settle down," Mr. Danza said. "Sam, you're on drinks. Eddie, get the paper plates. Trey, Manny, give them some help. You guys know the drill."

Sam's dad put the pizza boxes on the coffee table and the Cowboys surged forward. "Take it easy," Mr. Danza said. "There's plenty for everybody." Then he smiled and added with a shout, "Plenty for the only undefeated team in the Woodside Football League!"

Instantly the Cowboys started another chant and broke into rhythmic clapping. "Undefeated." *Clap...clap...clap-clap-clap.* "Undefeated." *Clap...clap...clap-clap-clap.*

"Are we really the only undefeated team?" Manny asked.

"Yep." Sam handed out a sheet of paper to each of his teammates. "I made copies of the standings from the league website this morning," he said as the boys studied the team names and records.

Team	W	L	T
Cowboys	6	0	0
Giants	5	1	0
Eagles	4	2	0
Panthers	4	2	0
Patriots	3	3	0
Jets	2	3	1
Bengals	2	4	0
Lions	2	4	0
Steelers	1	4	1
Seahawks	0	6	0

"We play the Bengals tomorrow," Trey said, pointing to the standings. "We'd better be ready."

Manny shrugged. "They're only 2–4."

"Yeah, but they gave the Giants a tough game," Sam reminded him.

"We've only got to beat them and one more team, and then we'll be league champs," Trey said.

The Cowboys linemen, sitting together on the couch, started chanting and clapping again.

"Undefeated…undefeated…undefeated…"

Mr. Danza held up his hands for quiet. "Okay, guys," he said. "I'm going to start the video. Then I've got to go out for about an hour to run some errands." He gave everyone in the room a serious look. "No horsing around."

"We'll be fine," Sam said.

"Okay, be good. And pick up. I don't want to see a mess when I get back." Mr. Danza paused at the door and turned around. "Enjoy the game," he said. "I'm sure you will."

The Cowboys cheered and then settled in for the game. Watching from his father's leather chair, Sam could see that every play was hard fought. He could almost feel each block and tackle coming through the screen. He remembered how battered and tired he had felt. But he also remembered how proud he had been of the Cowboys through all the back-and-forth of the game. They had hung tough and played like a real team.

Finally it was time for the Cowboys' final drive.

"Watch closely, guys," Trey said, standing in the middle of the room. "And observe how a two-minute drill is supposed to be run."

"Sit down," Manny called from the couch. "Watch the blocking. You can't run a two-minute drill without blocking."

Trey sat down but started to call out the plays at the screen. "Here's a quick pass to Jared!"

On the screen, Jared caught the ball and the Cowboys cheered.

"All right, Jared."

"Clutch grab."

"Good hands."

"Okay, now we're moving!" Trey shouted. "Let's give it to my man Sam."

Sam watched his run and remembered his decision to get out of bounds. The room filled with cheers again.

"Way to get out of bounds."

"Stop the clock, dude. Stop the clock."

"Sam, you ran great all game," Trey said. "Must have been that scooter saving your legs."

Sam laughed. "Yeah, I'm the Scooter Man."

The plays kept coming. Sam and his teammates leaned closer to the screen.

"Watch this perfect pass," Trey said, pretending to throw a pass across the room. Jared stretched and caught the ball on the screen.

"First and ten at the twelve," Trey shouted as he traded high fives with Jared.

The plays piled up in a blur of action.

Eddie's run, no gain. The fumble. Sam almost leaped out of his chair the moment the ball popped loose. "Man, we were *so* lucky on that play," he said under his breath.

Sam's short run.

The quick pass to Jared.

By now all the Cowboys were up and shouting at the screen. Some were counting down the final seconds. Trey was shouting out the play just like he had in the game.

"I-38...I-38... I-38..."

"Three...two..."

Sam suddenly slumped back in his father's chair. His heart was pounding and he struggled to catch his breath. But it wasn't the memory of his big touchdown that was making him feel so sick. It was something else. Something none of the other Cowboys had noticed. Something *no one* had noticed.

On the television screen, the ball was snapped. Sam ran to the right and, with his last ounce of energy, lunged across the goal for the score. The Cowboys jumped around and cheered in Sam's family room just as they had in the Giants end zone. Everyone except Sam. He sat completely still in his father's leather chair, staring blankly ahead. Finally he jumped up and grabbed the remote control from the coffee table. "Wait a minute, wait a minute!" he shouted above the noise, fumbling with the remote.

"What's your problem?" Trey asked in disbelief. "Are you crazy?"

"I didn't score," Sam said, still unable to make the remote work. The nightmare was still on the screen.

Everyone in the room froze.

"*What?*" Trey said, frowning.

Sam stared at the remote. He took a deep breath and looked up at his silent teammates.

"I didn't score."

Chapter 9

"Huh? What are you talking about, Scooter Man?" Trey said. "You just saw the play. You got the ball over the goal line."

"Yeah," agreed Manny. "The Cowboys are totally undefeated!" He gave a quick air-punch that fired up everyone again.

"Undefeated...undefeated...undefeated!" they chanted.

But Sam wasn't listening. He was busy with the remote, rewinding the video and scanning the action blurring by on the TV. "That's not what I'm talking about. I know I got over the goal line," he said in a tight, tense voice.

The chanting stopped.

"Hey, the ref signaled the touchdown," Eddie said, trying to be helpful.

"After a great block by me," Manny added proudly.

But Sam just kept studying the TV. Finally he hit the stop button and turned to his teammates. "I scored on the *fifth* down," he said quietly.

"You've gone crazy, Scooter Man," Trey said, trying to joke. "The down marker on the last play said it was fourth down. I remember looking—"

"The down marker was wrong!" Sam snapped before Trey finished talking.

"Come on, Sam," Trey said, taking the remote. "Forget about it. We won!"

"Whoa! Sam, are you saying that the last touchdown shouldn't have counted?" Eddie asked.

Sam turned toward his friend. "Yes," he said. "That's exactly what I'm saying."

"Wait a sec," Manny said hopefully. "Didn't we get a first down on that quick pass over the middle?"

"Yeah," said Trey. "I'm sure we got a first down on that play."

"No," Sam said as he grabbed the remote back from Trey and pressed the play button. All the players turned their attention to the TV as Sam ran the crucial plays in slow motion. "See, there's the long pass to Jared that gave us a first down," Sam said.

"Where did they put down the ball?" Eddie asked, leaning forward.

"On the 12-yard line," Sam said, pointing at the referee on the screen.

"So what?" Manny shrugged.

"So we have to get the ball to the two-yard line to get a first down," Sam said.

Trey patted Manny on the head as if Manny were a little kid. "It takes ten yards to get a first down. I thought even linemen knew that."

Manny knocked Trey's hand away from his head.

"Watch the TV," Sam ordered.

Sam didn't have to tell the Cowboys to pay attention. Every eye was glued to the TV. No one said a word or even took a bite of pizza as the final plays of the game flashed across the screen.

The quick handoff to Eddie.

The fumble.

Another run by Sam.

The quick pass to Jared.

Sam's touchdown.

Five plays, five downs. There was no doubt about it: The referee had given the Cowboys an extra down. Sam's touchdown was no good.

"In all the confusion and running around," Sam said, "the guy with the down marker must have forgotten to change the down on one of the plays."

"Look," Eddie said as the Cowboys watched the series of five plays again. "Sam's right. The down marker says it's second down, but it's really third down."

Sam pointed the remote at the screen after the quick pass to Jared. "See, that pass play only got us to the three-yard line, so, it wasn't a first down." He shook his head and added, "It should have been the Giants' ball after that pass play."

Trey looked at the ceiling and started to laugh.

"What's so funny?" Sam demanded.

"Those Giants are so dumb," Trey said, still laughing. "They can't even count."

Manny grinned at Trey. "And their coaches can't count either!" he said.

The two boys traded high fives.

"But we didn't win," Sam insisted. "We got an extra down. We got a fifth down."

"So what?" Trey said. "Will you relax, Scooter Man? The refs didn't say anything. The Giants didn't even protest the game. It's been almost a week."

"Yeah," Manny agreed. "The Giants coaches didn't say anything. I guess they count like this: One...two...*two*...three... four."

A few of the other Cowboys laughed too.

"I don't know," Eddie said slowly, breaking the happy mood. "It doesn't seem right, scoring on a fifth down."

Trey glared at him. "What are you talking about?"

Before Eddie could answer, Sam said, "Yeah, it seems like it's cheating or something."

Trey's eyes blazed into Sam. "You've got to be kidding," he said.

Sam kept his voice steady. "It feels like we're taking something that doesn't belong to us," he said.

"You mean like that scooter you found?" Trey snapped. "*Beside* the trash barrel?"

Sam felt like he'd been blindsided by a tackle. He didn't say anything, but he knew that Trey was right. It was exactly like taking that scooter.

"Why are you guys always talking about that stupid scooter?" Manny asked.

Sam didn't answer. He quickly tried to get the conversation back on track. "Maybe we should tell somebody about the game," he said, avoiding Trey's stare.

"We could tell your dad, Trey," Eddie said. "He's the coach."

"Are you kidding?" Trey scoffed. "I know what my dad would say."

"What?"

"He'd say that the refs made the calls. Sam scored the touchdown and we won." Trey looked back at Sam. "Don't you want to be the big hero?"

"Yeah, but—"

"My dad wanted to beat the Giants more than anybody," Trey broke in.

"You think Brady and the Giants would care if *they* scored on a fifth down?" Manny asked.

"Nope," Trey said. "And Sam, Brady's the guy who almost killed you in that touch football game. Remember? He started the fight in PE, too."

Sam looked around the room. Some of his teammates were nodding. But other players looked confused, as if they didn't know what to think. The room started to buzz with the boys talking to each other in whispers.

Sam thought back to when he was sitting in Mr. Hanley's office with Brady. "Brady stood up for me after we got in that fight in gym," he said. "So I don't know. Maybe Brady and the Giants *would* do something if they scored on a fifth down."

Trey and some of the Cowboys traded glances.

"Well, I just think we should do something," Eddie spoke up.

"Yeah," Trey said. "We should do some-thing, all right. We should keep our mouths shut. We won!" He turned off the TV. "We should go out and beat the Bengals tomor-row afternoon and stay undefeated." He thrust his fist into the air and chanted, "Undefeated...undefeated...undefeated..."

The Cowboys joined in, clapping and chanting.

But as Sam looked around the room, he noticed that some of the Cowboys weren't clapping and chanting at all.

Chapter 10

The next morning, Sam sat up in bed the moment his alarm went off. He dressed quickly in his usual jeans, sneakers, and sweatshirt and tiptoed down the stairs.

"Hey, Sam, where are you going?"

"Huh?" Sam spun toward the direction of the voice. "Oh. Dad," he said, letting out his breath. "Hi."

His dad was on the living room floor, doing his morning sit-ups. "What are you up to, Sam?"

"Um, I forgot to tell you that, I, ah, was going to go down to the park early this morning."

"What? At eight o'clock on a Saturday? I thought you were going to sleep in." His father sounded confused. "You've got a game later today."

"Yeah, I know," Sam said. "I just need to practice a few plays. But I won't be long."

"What about breakfast?"

"I'll eat later."

"Okay then," his dad said, and started doing more sit-ups.

Sam quietly got his scooter from the hall closet and slipped out the door.

A few clouds hung low in the sky as Sam glided off on the scooter. Rain had been forecast, but hopefully it wouldn't start until after their game against the Bengals. For now, the cool air felt good and Sam enjoyed rolling through the empty streets. It seemed as if everyone was sleeping in except him.

But as he got closer to the center of town, the streets grew more crowded. He hopped the curb with his feet tight on the scooter and coasted down the sidewalk. A block away, a large sign that read "Police Station" hung on a plain, two-story brick building.

Sam carried the scooter up the front steps and pulled it along a short hallway. The station was quiet, except for an officer sitting at a computer behind a long counter. Sam was almost too nervous to speak, but he managed to say, "Um, excuse me."

The officer looked up. "May I help you?" she asked.

The words tumbled out so fast, Sam hardly knew what he was saying: "I want to turn in some stolen property. *I* didn't steal it...I mean, I didn't mean to...I mean, maybe nobody stole it. The brakes don't work too well."

"Slow down, young man," the officer said. The gold metal name tag on her dark blue uniform said "Sergeant Sharon Jones." "What do you have there?" she asked.

Sam leaned back and looked down. "This scooter," he said, pointing.

Sergeant Jones leaned over the counter and looked down. "So it's not your scooter?"

"Well...no. I mean, kind of. I found it."

"Okay," Sergeant Jones said. "Where did you find it?"

"By a trash can. In the parking lot near the North Woodside field. It was after my football practice."

"And what day was that?"

"Thursday."

"Last Thursday?"

"No, a week ago.

"A week ago?" Sergeant Jones said, sounding surprised.

Sam could feel himself sweating. "Yes. But I didn't steal it. I mean, I thought somebody didn't want it anymore because it was leaning against the trash can."

The officer walked around the counter. "Let me take a look at it," she said as Sam handed her the scooter. "Pretty nice," she observed.

"The brakes don't work so well," Sam reminded her.

Sergeant Jones wasn't really listening, though. She turned the scooter upside down and looked at the bottom. "Here it is," she said. "This is a weird place for it."

"For what?"

"The owner registration number," she said, pointing to a series of small numbers. She grabbed a memo pad from the counter and wrote down the number. Then she pointed her pen to a chair against the wall.

"Sit down over there, please," she said. "I'll be back in a minute."

Sam pulled the scooter over to the chair and sat down, feeling a little bit like he was sitting outside Mr. Hanley's office. He could hear Sergeant Jones on the phone, but it was hard to tell what she was saying. Finally she returned, smiling.

"Well, I found the owner," she declared.

"You did? Who is it?" Sam asked.

"A boy who lives two blocks from here. I told his mother I'd bring it to him." Sergeant Jones turned to another officer who had just walked into the room. "Will you cover the desk for a little while, Gerard? We have to return some lost property." Then she turned to Sam. "Do you want to come with me?"

Sam hesitated. He wasn't sure he wanted to hang out with a police officer.

Before he could answer her first question, she asked, "By the way, do your parents know you're out this early?"

"Yes," said Sam. "My dad does."

"Well, come on, then. You can ride the scooter over there."

"That's okay," Sam said. "I think I'll just carry it." He folded up the scooter and put it under his arm.

He felt a little strange walking down the street with a police officer. He was glad it was still early in the morning and most people were still inside. "How did you find out who owned it?" Sam asked.

"You know that owner's registration decal on the bottom? I looked up the number," Sergeant Jones said. "It had been reported missing, so I called the owner."

As they turned a corner, Sam saw a boy about eight years old and his mom standing in their front yard. The boy started running toward them. Sam quickly unfolded the scooter and held it steady on the sidewalk.

"My scooter!" the boy cried out in delight. He grabbed the scooter from Sam's hands and hopped on. He barely noticed Sergeant Jones or Sam.

"Be careful, Nathan," his mom called. But the boy was already sailing down the sidewalk.

"Thank you so much. Where did you find it?" she asked Sergeant Jones.

"I didn't," Sergeant Jones said, tapping Sam on the shoulder. "This young man brought it in."

"So where did you find it?" Nathan's mother repeated, this time to Sam. "We've looked everywhere for that scooter."

"Over near North Woodside Park," Sam said.

The woman looked surprised. "Really?" she said. "My goodness, I wonder how it got way over there."

"My guess," said Sergeant Jones, "is that someone stole it from your house, took it for a joyride across town, and ditched it at the park."

Nathan's mom nodded and took a couple of dollars from her jeans pocket. "Well, thank you for bringing it back," she said to Sam. "My son loves that scooter. I'd like to give you a reward."

"That's okay," Sam said. "I didn't do anything."

"You turned it in to the police station," she said, holding out the money. "You could have kept it."

"No, really, thanks," Sam said quickly. He looked at the younger boy gliding happily back toward them on his shiny scooter. "I don't need a reward."

Sam could hear the rain hitting his helmet as he stood in the Cowboys huddle. It had been raining for two hours straight. The ground was soggy and Sam's rain-soaked uniform was heavy. His hands were wet and cold. A gray October mist hovered along the edge of the field.

The Cowboys were playing as if their brains were in a fog, too. Sam gazed through the mist at the yellow lights of the scoreboard.

The Cowboys and the Bengals were tied 6–6 with five minutes to play.

"Come on, let's get moving!" Trey shouted, clapping his hands and returning to the huddle from a sideline conference with Coach Johnson. "We should be killing these guys."

Sam and Eddie traded glances in the huddle. Sam knew that Eddie was thinking the same thing: The Cowboys didn't seem to have the same spirit after Friday night's fifth-down discussion. Trey and Manny and a few of the other guys were playing hard, but the rest of the team seemed sluggish, as if they were sleepwalking through the game.

"All right, I-35 on two," Trey snapped. "And let's give Sam some blocking."

"Ready…set…hut…hut."

The Cowboys line moved forward in the mud and muck. Sam took the handoff and saw a small hole between the Cowboys left guard and tackle. He tried to break through, but his cleats kept slipping on the wet turf. He hit the line, pushing past the players' hands and arms slapping against his soaking uniform and skin. Finally he tripped and skidded in the mud for a six-yard gain.

Back in the huddle, Trey tried to get the team pumped up. But Sam wasn't sure even the Cowboys' star quarterback could do that.

"Good run," Trey said, clapping his hands. "Let's try the other side this time. I-34 on one."

Sam slipped and slid for another six-yard gain behind a good block by Eddie.

"First down," the referee said, pointing down the field.

"Let's keep it on the ground," Trey said. "I-22. Eddie right up the middle."

This time the Bengals defense got through and stopped Eddie after a gain of only two yards.

On the next play Sam tried a sweep to the right, but slipped on the wet field and fell on his back for no gain. It was third down and eight yards to go. Time was running out. The rain fell even harder.

"Time out!" Trey shouted and ran to the

sidelines to talk quickly with his dad.

The Cowboys knelt in a circle in the mud. Sam could feel the ooze of the field puddling around his knee. But he didn't care. Every inch of him was already soaking wet.

Eddie was kneeling beside Sam. "A tie isn't so bad," he said. "We'll still be ahead of the Giants."

"Yeah, unless we give the fifth-down game to the Giants," Sam said, lowering his voice and tilting his head so only his friend could hear. "Then we won't have any chance to win the league championship." Sam looked up into the rain and the dark gray sky. "Third down and eight," he said. "I don't think we can pass the ball in the rain."

"Tough day to run the ball, too," Eddie said.

Sam wiped his face with his wet shirt. "It's a tough day to do anything," he said.

Trey ran back into the huddle. The Cowboys stood and snapped their chin straps tight. "Listen up," Trey said. "This is a big play. Let's run a fake I-37, quarterback bootleg right. On one."

Trey looked at Sam. "You've got to really sell the fake on the handoff."

Sam lined up behind Eddie in the Cowboys backfield. *This play might work,* he thought. *If the Bengals think I have the ball and start chasing me, it'll be hard for them to turn around in the mud and go after Trey.*

"Ready...set...hut."

Sam and the Cowboys moved left as if they were going to run a sweep to that side. Trey dropped back a couple of steps like he was handing off the ball to Sam. Trying his best to fake out the Bengals, Sam closed his hands over an imaginary ball. But at the last instant Trey pivoted with the ball and started running to the right.

The Bengals team charged hard toward Sam. When they realized they'd been fooled, they turned sharply to change direction, but some players slipped and fell on the wet grass. Others were easily knocked down by the Cowboys linemen.

Trey dodged an oncoming tackler and broke into the clear, splashing down the right sideline to the goal line. He was at the 30-yard line…25…20…

Some Bengals defensive backs raced after him, but they didn't have a chance.

He was at the 15…10…5…

Trey was going all the way. Eddie, Jared, Manny, and the other Cowboys ran down the field, jumping and celebrating in the rain. Sam cheered too. He still felt funny about the Giants game, but he would rather win a game than lose it on such a dreary, wet Saturday.

Eddie blasted over for the two-point conversion. The Cowboys led 14–6.

"Great job, guys! Just hold them for a few downs!" Coach Johnson shouted from the sidelines, shaking both fists. "We've got this one."

Fired up by Trey's touchdown run, the Cowboys stopped the Bengals cold on the final plays. A few minutes later the Cowboys ran off the field, sweating and caked with mud, but winners.

Trey was the happiest Cowboy of all. He pulled off his helmet, then threw one arm around Sam's neck and the other around Eddie's. "Tough game," he said, "but we're still undefeated!" The rain splashed against the top of Trey's head and ran in tiny streams down his face.

"Yeah," Eddie said. "If we win next week, we win the championship!" He shot a quick glance at Sam, who smiled but said nothing.

Sam wasn't thinking about how the Cowboys would win their next game. He was still thinking about the Giants game— and the illegal fifth down.

Chapter 12

Sam clicked off the TV and the room went dark. "So that's the deal, Dad," Sam said. "We won that game on the fifth down. It's really the Giants who should be undefeated."

Mr. Danza flicked on the side table lamp in the den. It was Friday, the night before the Cowboys' last game, and the rest of the team hadn't arrived yet for pizza. Mr. Danza sat back in his chair, frowning at the blank screen. "I can't believe it," he said. "I never realized..."

"Everything was happening so fast," Sam said.

His dad nodded. "I guess nobody noticed."

"Nobody except your camera," Sam said,

motioning toward the video camera on his father's desk in the corner.

"Yeah, I guess I'm the only parent crazy enough to film every game," Mr. Danza said, sounding almost embarrassed. Then he looked up. "Do the other guys on the team know about this?" he asked.

Sam nodded. "We all watched the film a couple of times," he said. "Last week when you went out to do errands."

"Well, what did they say?"

"Trey thinks we shouldn't say anything. He says his dad would say the same thing."

"And what do you think?" Mr. Danza asked.

Sam took a deep breath. "I don't know." He paused. "But it doesn't seem right to win on a fifth down. It's kind of like taking something that doesn't belong to us."

Mr. Danza looked at his watch. "The team will be here in a few minutes," he said. "You should talk it over with them."

"I don't know what good that will do," Sam said. "We've already talked it over."

Mr. Danza put his fingertips together

and looked at Sam for a moment. The Cowboys would be at the door any minute, and Sam had no idea what he would say to them.

Finally Mr. Danza said, "Maybe I can help."

"Really? How?"

"Tell you what," Mr. Danza said, getting out of his chair and moving toward the TV. "I'll show the end of the Giants game again. And then I'll tell you all a story I know about football."

Sam gave his father a doubtful look. He wasn't so sure that the team needed to hear one of his dad's old stories.

"Really," Mr. Danza said. "I think it will help."

In a few minutes everything seemed the same as any other Friday night. Sam's teammates arrived, grabbed their pizza and drinks, and settled in groups around the TV.

"Maybe we shouldn't even watch the Bengals game," Manny said.

"Yeah, we pretty much stunk," Eddie agreed.

"Are you kidding me?" Trey blurted out. "I want to see my great touchdown run."

"Why don't you hit the lights?" Mr. Danza said to Sam.

The room went dark and Mr. Danza started the game video. But it wasn't the Bengals film. It was the end of the Giants game.

"Hey, this isn't the Bengals game," Trey muttered.

"I know," Mr. Danza said. "It's just the last few plays of the Giants game. I want to check on something."

No one said a word as the final plays flickered across the screen, but Sam could see a few of the Cowboys squirming in their seats.

The quick handoff to Eddie.

The fumble.

Another run by Sam.

The quick pass to Jared.

And finally, Sam's touchdown.

Five plays. Five downs.

This time, as Sam plunged forward for the winning touchdown on screen there were no cheers in the room. The only sound was Trey stirring the ice in his cup with his finger. Mr. Danza stopped the film and the team sat very still in the dark. After what seemed like forever, the lights finally came back on. Mr. Danza stood in front of the team. Sam noticed that most of the Cowboys were looking down at the floor and not at his father.

Trey was studying Sam, and when their eyes locked Sam quickly looked away. He was glad he had told his dad about the fifth down, but having Trey stare at him that way made him feel like a traitor.

"Guys, I'm going to tell you a story," Mr. Danza began, "about a football game that happened a long time ago."

Trey shifted his gaze to Sam's dad. "What's that game got to do with us?" he asked.

"Let me tell the story," Mr. Danza said. "And then you can decide."

"When did the game happen?" Sam asked.

His dad smiled. "November 1940," he said. "A long, long time ago."

"Who played?" Eddie chimed in.

"It was Dartmouth College and Cornell University."

"They aren't very good at football," Trey scoffed.

Sam's dad raised his eyebrows. "Actually, Trey, Cornell was the number one team in the country back then."

"Cornell?" Manny asked in disbelief. "You're kidding."

"Nope," Mr. Danza continued. "Cornell was undefeated. In fact, Cornell hadn't lost a game in more than two years. In their last eighteen games, they had one tie and seventeen wins."

Sam noticed that even Trey looked impressed.

"Anyway, it was snowing that day and Dartmouth was putting up a real fight," Mr. Danza went on. "They led Cornell 3–0 late in the second half. In the final few minutes, Cornell got the ball around midfield and started driving downfield as the seconds ticked away."

Sam could see his teammates leaning

forward, listening. Sam's father was a good storyteller.

"Cornell had no time-outs left. So the referees were hurrying to get the ball back for the snap after every play. Just like the referees were doing at the Giants game."

Sam caught Trey's eye. They could both sense where the story was heading.

"In the confusion and in the snow, the refs lost track of the downs." Sam's father paused and looked around the room. "On the last play of the game, the referees gave Cornell an extra down—a fifth down—by mistake." Mr. Danza stopped.

"So what happened?" Trey asked.

"Cornell scored on the last play—the fifth down—and won the game." Mr. Danza paused again.

"That's it?" Sam asked, surprised. "That's the end of the story?"

"Not quite," his father replied. "When the Cornell team checked the game film, they saw the referee's mistake. They saw they had scored on a fifth down."

"So what did they do?" Manny asked.

Mr. Danza looked around the room. Every eye was fixed on him. The Cowboys barely seemed to be breathing.

"The Cornell team took a vote and they decided to give the game to Dartmouth."

"They gave the game to the other team?" Trey said, sounding shocked.

Mr. Danza nodded. "They gave the win to Dartmouth." He waited, giving every one of the Cowboys a chance to think about what the Cornell team had done. Then he said, "Maybe you guys should take a vote, like the Cornell team did."

Some of the Cowboys squirmed in their seats. "You have two choices," Mr. Danza suggested softly. "Keep the win and don't tell anyone about the fifth down—or give the game to the Giants."

Okay, let's talk it over," Sam said, looking around the den. Most of the Cowboys were just looking at each other. It seemed as if nobody wanted to be the first to speak.

"What's there to talk about?" Trey said, his voice getting louder as he spoke. "We won. The Giants lost. We're undefeated and tomorrow we have a chance to win it all."

"Yeah, but—" Eddie started.

"But what?" Trey said, spinning to look straight at Eddie. "The refs made the call. We didn't break any rules. We're not going to give the game to the Giants."

"The Cornell guys did," Sam said.

"That was a long time ago," Trey shot back.

"That doesn't mean they didn't do it," Sam answered.

"It's different now—"

"How?" Sam asked, starting to feel more confident.

"Well, now people want to win—"

"Cornell was undefeated. They hadn't lost a game in two years! "

"Maybe they didn't want to win badly enough," Trey said.

"I think maybe we should give the game to the Giants," Manny said, sitting on the couch in the middle of the Cowboys linemen. He had been quiet most of the evening. Now he seemed ready to talk.

Everyone in the room shifted slightly to watch Trey and Manny.

"*What?*" Trey shouted in disbelief. "You don't want to win? You don't want to beat the Giants?"

"I didn't say that," Manny said

"Look, the mistake happened to both teams," Trey insisted. "Remember, the

Giants thought it was fourth down, too."

"But it was *fifth* down," Sam and Manny said at the same time.

Trey changed direction, as if he were trying to shake a tackler. "Well, maybe we would have done things differently...called another play...if we'd thought we didn't have another down," he said.

"That doesn't change things," Manny said. "We still scored on the fifth down."

Trey looked disgusted.

Manny shrugged. "Hey, I may be a lineman," he said, "but even I know that it isn't right."

"Hey, come on. It's official. We won. We're undefeated," Trey pleaded.

"Yeah, we're undefeated," Sam said, "*if* we really won."

His words hung in the silence.

"We can't just give the game to the Giants," Trey protested. Then he turned and glared at Sam. "Anyway, maybe you should give back that scooter you *found* before you start telling us what to do."

Sam was ready. "I already gave it back."

"Oh yeah? When?"

"Last Saturday," he said. "It belonged to a kid on Dale Drive."

"What are you guys talking about?" Mr. Danza asked from the corner of the room.

"Nothing," Sam said quickly.

"Okay, why don't we vote?" Eddie suggested. He sounded impatient.

"Fine, we'll vote," Trey agreed.

"A couple of guys aren't here," Jared pointed out.

"We've got enough," Trey said.

"Are we voting in front of everybody?" Jared asked.

Sam hadn't thought about that. For the first time he realized he wasn't sure how Jared or most of the other Cowboys would vote.

Sam's father stood up. "Tell you what," he said, grabbing a notebook and a pile of pens from his desk. "You guys can each write down your vote on a piece of paper." He walked around the den handing out pens and slips of paper. "That way nobody will know how anyone else voted," he said.

The players took the pens and paper. Sam noticed that his teammates were glancing sideways at each other as if they were wondering what everyone else was going to do.

Mr. Danza stood in the middle of the room and held up his hands. "All right, the team is voting on whether you should give the game to the Giants because you scored on a fifth down," he announced.

"So if you write yes on the paper," Sam explained, "you want to give the win to the Giants."

"And if you write no," Trey added quickly, "that means you think we should keep the win."

"Everybody got it?" Mr. Danza asked.

"We got it," Manny said.

"Do we have to vote one way or another?" one of the reserves asked.

"You've got to vote," Sam said. "Either yes or no."

He counted the players in the room. Fifteen. That meant there couldn't be a tie vote. The Cowboys would decide tonight.

The players started to write down their votes. Some covered their papers with their hands. Everyone folded their papers several times into neat, small squares. Mr. Danza went around the room with an upturned baseball cap and each player dropped his paper into the cap.

"Okay, has everybody voted?"

All of the boys nodded.

"Who wants to read out the votes?" Mr. Danza asked.

"I will," Sam said, raising his hand as if he were in school.

Mr. Danza reached into the cap and handed Sam the first vote. Sam unfolded the paper and read the vote to the group.

"Yes."

"Let me see that," Trey said.

"Don't you trust your own teammate?" Sam asked, frowning.

"I'm just checking," Trey said.

Sam handed the paper to Trey. "Here, look," he said.

Trey saw that it said yes and nodded.

The count continued in the same pattern:

Mr. Danza pulled a vote from the cap, then Sam read it aloud, and handed it to Trey.

"Yes."

"No."

"Yes."

"No."

"No."

"Yes."

Sam smiled at one vote when he recognized Eddie's handwriting. He knew he could count on his friend.

"Yes."

"Yes."

"No."

"What's the score?" Manny asked.

"Six to four," Trey answered. "The yes votes are ahead."

"There are five votes left," Mr. Danza said as he handed another piece of paper to Sam.

"No."

Trey pumped his fist into the air. The rest of the Cowboys didn't move.

Sam opened another folded paper.

"No."

By now it seemed as if the entire team was holding its breath. Sam could feel his hands shake as he opened the next vote.

"Yes."

Sam fumbled even more with the next piece of paper.

"No."

The count was tied—seven yes votes, seven no votes. The next vote would decide. Mr. Danza handed Sam the last piece of paper and turned the cap right side up to show everyone that there were no more votes in the cap.

The Cowboys leaned forward. Sam took a deep breath and shut his eyes for a moment. He unfolded the paper and saw a single, carefully printed word.

"Yes."

Trey fell back into the chair as if he'd been tackled by a blitzing linebacker. "I can't believe it," he groaned. "We could have been undefeated!"

"Yes, but the vote was fair," Mr. Danza said. "The team voted to give the win to the Giants. I'll call Coach Johnson and see how he wants to break the news to the Giants coach. Then we'll e-mail the league." Mr. Danza headed toward the door. "You guys watch the film of the Bengals game."

Trey stood up. "I'm not watching the stupid Bengals game," he said as he snatched his jacket from the couch.

"Come on, Trey," Sam said. "The team voted fair and square."

"Yeah," Manny said. "Don't you want to see your touchdown run?"

"I don't care about any touchdown run," Trey said. "And I don't want to hang out with a bunch of guys who don't want to win."

Time to get up." Sam's head popped up off his pillow when he heard the knock on the door and his father's voice. Mr. Danza stepped over the dirty clothes scattered on the bedroom floor and raised the shade to let in the bright autumn sunshine. The sudden flood of light made Sam blink. But his eyes quickly adjusted and settled on the football uniform he had hung neatly on the back of a chair last night. His shoulder pads and helmet were laid out on the seat of the chair.

"What time is it?" Sam asked, already thinking ahead to today's game.

"Around ten o'clock. I let you sleep late. I figured you were tired." Mr. Danza handed

Sam a single sheet of paper. "The league posted a special announcement on the website early this morning about the Giants game," he said.

Sam propped himself up, wiped the sleep from his eyes, and read the bulletin.

SPECIAL ANNOUNCEMENT!

The commissioner of the Woodside Football League has declared that the score of the game between the Cowboys and the Giants was incorrectly recorded. After reviewing film of the game, which was submitted by the Cowboys, the commissioner has determined that the Cowboys' final touchdown did not count. The officials made an incorrect call, as the touchdown was scored on a fifth down. The ball should have gone to the Giants after the fourth down. The commissioner has now declared the Giants the winners of that game. The score will be recorded as Giants 16, Cowboys 12.

Due to the correction of the final score of the Giants/Cowboys game, the official standings for the Woodside Football League have changed. See chart for current standings:

Team	W	L	T
Giants	7	0	0
Cowboys	6	1	0
Panthers	5	2	0
Eagles	4	3	0
Lions	3	4	0
Patriots	3	4	0
Jets	2	4	1
Bengals	2	5	0
Steelers	1	5	1
Seahawks	1	6	0

Sam fell back onto his bed and stared at the ceiling. Now the team's vote to give the game to the Giants seemed all too real. His father patted him on the shoulder. "Come on, get up and get ready. I'll make you breakfast," he said. "The only way you guys have a chance to tie for the championship is to beat the Lions today."

Sam lay still for a long while. Then he grabbed the announcement and stared at the standings again. He could hardly believe that his team was now in second place, a game behind the Giants.

A few hours later Sam and Eddie arrived at the football field. "Hey, Trey," Sam said, spotting the Cowboys quarterback. "Did you see the announcement from the league?"

"Yeah, I saw it," Trey said.

"What did your dad think?" Eddie asked.

"I think he wished we'd kept our mouths shut," Trey said, looking across the field. "But he figured if the team voted to give the game to the Giants, he had to go along with our decision." Trey still seemed upset.

"You ready to play today?" Sam asked.

"Yeah, sure," Trey said. "But I don't think we're playing for much."

"What do you mean?" Eddie said. "The Giants could lose today and then we'd have a chance to tie them for the championship."

"Yeah, they play the Jets right after our game," Sam added. "We should stick around and cheer for the Jets."

"The Jets don't have a chance," Trey said. "Their best player got hurt last week. Derek Drake's not playing."

Sam's shoulders slumped. Trey was right. Without Derek, the Jets would need a miracle to score against the Giants.

The Cowboys-Lions game started off slowly, with the Cowboys struggling on the field. The lines were a step too slow. The handoffs and passes were not crisp and confident. Standing in the middle of the field, Sam could sense that something wasn't right. It was as if the Cowboys weren't thinking about the game. It was more like they were still thinking about last night's yes and no votes. Late in the first half the score was tied 0–0 when the Lions offense started moving down the field.

"Come on, guys!" Sam shouted, trying to pump up the Cowboys defense. "We gotta stop 'em. Let's get tough!" No one else said a word, but on the third down Manny quickly flattened the Lions runner. It was fourth down and less than a yard to go for the first down. The Lions decided to go for it and, for the first time in the game, the Cowboys huddle showed some of their usual spirit.

"We can hold them."

"Need a big play, defense."

"Come on, Cowboys!"

Both teams hustled to their positions. Sam crept a little closer to the line of scrimmage. He was hoping to make a big play to get his team going again. The Lions quarterback called out the signals: "Ready...set...hut...hut."

Sam sprinted forward to stop the run as the Lions quarterback handed the ball off to their running back.

"No!" Sam shouted as he skidded to a stop. The running play was a fake. The Lions quarterback had kept the ball and stepped back to pass. The Lions tight end burst past the line and sprinted up the middle of the field, right where Sam was supposed to be.

Sam turned and raced back. But it was too late. The Lions tight end caught the easy pass and ran, untouched, into the end zone.

The Lions scored the two-point conversion. The Cowboys, now trailing 8–0, trudged back up the field to receive the kickoff.

"Give me a good block," Sam whispered to Eddie as they waited for the kick. "I'm gonna run this one back for a touchdown."

The kickoff flew end over end to Sam at the ten-yard line. After a quick basket catch, Sam charged forward into a wall of tacklers. He kept his long legs churning and spun free of his attackers. Spying an opening in the field, he sprinted toward that daylight.

Suddenly Sam was running in the clear. A Lions defender angled toward him and dove at Sam's legs. Sam leaped over the tackler and stumbled just inside the sideline, but kept his balance. After a couple of quick steps he was running at top speed again. He was going all the way!

He made it to the 40-yard line...30... 20...10... Touchdown! Sam spiked the ball as hard as he could in the end zone. *That should get us fired up*, he thought as he jogged back to the sidelines.

But the Cowboys didn't score on the two-point conversion after Sam's touchdown. They still trailed the Lions at halftime, 8–6.

During the break, Coach Johnson tried to encourage his team. "Listen, forget about the Giants game," he said as he paced in front of the players. "Let's win *this* game!"

No one said anything. Most of the Cowboys were looking at the ground.

"Trey!" Coach Johnson shouted, startling the Cowboys quarterback. "You were sleeping in the first half. Let's show some hustle out there."

Sam could see Trey's face burning. He had never heard the coach yell at his son that way.

"And that goes for the rest of you, too!" Coach shouted as he punched the air with an angry finger. "Sam...Manny...Eddie... all of you! Let's start playing some real football...like Cowboys!" He glanced down at his clipboard and started giving orders. "We get the ball at the beginning of the second half. Let's try to keep it on the ground and wear them down. Linemen, you gotta open some holes out there. Come on!"

Sam was fired up, but he wasn't sure that his team could pull things together enough to win. He jogged over to the water bucket to get a quick drink before the start of the second half.

"Hey, what's with you guys?" a familiar voice asked.

Sam turned to see Brady standing with a group of Giants on the sidelines. "Oh, hi," he said. "I guess we're just a little flat today."

Brady looked annoyed. "You should be killing the Lions," he said.

"I'm not so sure about that." Sam started guzzling the water from his plastic cup.

"Well, I am. You guys were the best team we played all year—by far." Then Brady looked back toward the Cowboys sideline and cupped his hands around his mouth. "Let's go, Cowboys!" he shouted.

The other Giants took up the chant and pounded out a series of loud claps.

"Let's go, Cowboys!"

Clap...clap...clap-clap-clap.

"Let's go, Cowboys!"

Clap…clap…clap-clap-clap.

"You're rooting for us?" Sam asked above the cheers.

"After what you guys did? Telling the league about the fifth down and giving us the game?" Brady said. "That took guts. You bet we're rooting for you."

Tweeeeet! The referee's whistle signaled the start of the second half.

"But we can still tie you guys for the championship," Sam said, jogging backward toward the field. "If we win today and you guys lose."

Brady waved away the idea. "Don't worry," he called after Sam. "We'll beat the Jets. You go beat the Lions."

Sam snapped his chin strap tight and ran to join his teammates for the kickoff. Brady and the Giants kept chanting and clapping on the sidelines.

"What's with those guys?" Trey asked, nodding toward the Giants as Sam leaned into the huddle.

"They're rooting for us," Sam said.

"Really?" Trey, Manny, and Eddie said all at once.

"Are they crazy?" Trey asked.

"Nope. Brady says we're the best team they played all year—by far."

Trey looked around the huddle as the Giants cheers echoed in the Cowboys' ears. "Well, let's show them they're right," he said.

After the kickoff, the Cowboys offense clicked into action. Eddie burst up the middle for a quick gain. Sam ran around the right end for a first down. Then he swept around the left end, dodging tacklers for another first down.

Suddenly the Cowboys were moving so quickly that the linesmen on the sideline had trouble keeping up. Brady and the Giants kept chanting and clapping.

"Let's go, Cowboys."

Clap...clap...clap-clap-clap.

A pass to Jared and two more runs moved the ball to the Lions 15-yard line.

Now the Cowboys were really fired up. "Come on!" Sam shouted in the huddle.

"Let's keep it going." The Giants cheers grew even louder.

"I-34, on one," Trey ordered. The team clapped in perfect unison and hustled into position. "Ready…set…hut!"

The play unfolded on the field just as it had been written in the Cowboys playbook. Sam took the handoff from Trey. Eddie blocked and Sam broke through the hole in the right side of the line. He sidestepped a Lion tackler and raced into the end zone.

Touchdown!

The entire Cowboys team was right behind Sam. They surrounded him in the end zone and pounded him on his helmet and shoulder pads.

With the cheers of both the Giants and his own teammates ringing in his ears, Sam smiled. At least the Cowboys hadn't given up.

They still had a chance.

Chapter 15

"Peet-*za*...peet-*za*...peet-*za*!" Mr. Danza walked into the family room, put down the pizza boxes, then asked, "Hey, where is everybody?"

Trey shrugged. "I guess some of the guys figured the season was over, so why bother watching the game?" he said.

Sam looked around the room, counting his teammates. "We've still got eleven," he said. "That's enough for a team."

"More pizza for you guys, then," Mr. Danza said, opening one of the boxes.

"We can have pizza for breakfast," Sam said with a grin.

"Do you still want to watch the Lions game?" Sam's father asked as the boys grabbed their plates and began munching on pizza.

"We were pretty lousy in the first half," Manny said.

"Hey, what about my big touchdown run on the kickoff?" Sam said.

"That was pretty cool," Eddie said. "And we played a lot better in the second half."

"Yeah, we finally got our act together. I can't believe we beat them 22-8!" Sam said.

"Hey, Mr. Danza," Trey said, his face lighting up. "Why don't we watch Sam's kickoff return and then fast-forward to the second half?"

Mr. Danza laughed. "Sounds like a plan."

Sam's father fiddled with the remote as the figures on the television screen flashed by at superspeed.

"Check that out!" Trey said, pointing at the speeded-up action on the screen. "Even Manny's running fast."

"At least I'm blocking," Manny retorted. "You never block—at any speed."

"Here's the runback," Mr. Danza said, pressing the play button.

The team broke into cheers as they watched Sam spin to the left and sprint down the sideline for the first-half touchdown.

"Great run," Eddie said.

"No thanks to you," Trey teased. "There was no blocking on that play."

"What about you, man?" Manny said. "You were out there too. Don't quarterbacks block?"

"We did okay," Trey responded.

"Yeah," Sam said, staring at the screen as the game fast-forwarded to the second half. "A 7–1 record is pretty good."

"Not as good as 8–0," Trey pointed out.

"True," Sam agreed. "You know, I figured things would turn out differently."

"What do you mean?" Trey asked.

Sam shrugged. "Well...we did the right thing by giving the game to the Giants," he said, then struggled to put his thoughts into words. "But I kind of thought we'd beat the Lions and...you know...the Jets would beat the Giants."

"Well *that* didn't happen," Trey said. "The Giants killed 'em, 30–0."

"I was kind of hoping the Giants might give the game back to us." Manny said.

"That didn't happen either," Trey said.

"Hey, Dad," Sam called across the room. "What happened to the Cornell team? You know, the one that voted to give the game to Dartmouth?"

Mr. Danza smiled. "They lost their next game to the University of Pennsylvania, 22–20. So they didn't win the championship, either."

"Kind of like us." Sam sighed.

"Hey, at least we won our last game," Trey said.

"Yeah, the Cornell team lost," Mr. Danza said. "But they're still remembered and admired for what they did." Then he looked around the room at all the boys and asked, "So are you still glad you voted to give the game to the Giants?"

"I guess so," Sam said. "But I'm not sure people will know about what we did the same way they know about Cornell."

"*You'll* know," Sam's dad said firmly. "And that's what counts."

"Yeah, and the Giants sure know," Eddie said. "Did you hear them all cheering in the second half?"

The team broke into cheers and claps, just like the Giants.

"Let's go, Cowboys."

Clap...clap...clap-clap-clap.

"Let's go, Cowboys."

Clap...clap...clap-clap-clap.

"Yeah, having the Giants cheer for us was cool," Trey said as the noise died down.

"Even for a guy who voted no?" Sam teased.

"How do you know I voted no?" Trey challenged Sam. "It was a secret ballot. Maybe I voted yes."

The Cowboys hooted and laughed.

"Give us a break, dude."

"You're kidding, right?"

"Didn't you walk out after the vote?"

"Okay, okay. Maybe I did vote no." Trey grinned and grabbed another slice of pizza.

"Hey!" Manny protested. "Stop hogging the pepperoni."

"Yeah. Gimme some," Jared said.

"Me too," Eddie said, jumping up off the floor.

Soon everybody was pulling slices from the box and wolfing down more pizza—too busy eating to talk. As Sam scooped up a string of extra cheese, he looked around the room and thought back over the season: the Giants game, the extra down, the scooter, the Cornell-Dartmouth story, and the Cowboys' vote. Sam was really proud of what they had all done—even if they hadn't won the championship.

But hanging out on Friday night with the Cowboys, laughing, eating pizza, and teasing Trey, Sam was proud of something else, too.

The Cowboys were still a team.

The Real Story

In November 1940, Cornell was the best college team in the country. The Cornell Big Red was a football powerhouse, just like the University of Southern California, Ohio State, and Oklahoma are today.

Led by Coach Carl Snavely, Cornell had gone undefeated in 1939 with a record of 8–0 (college teams played fewer games in the old days). Cornell had won its first six games of the 1940 season, crushing their opponents by a combined score of 181–13. If Cornell won its remaining two games against Dartmouth and the University of Pennsylvania, the Big Red would win its second straight national championship.

The game against Dartmouth on November 16 should have been an easy win for Cornell, even though Dartmouth was playing at home. Dartmouth's record was just three wins and four losses, and Big Red had beaten Dartmouth 35–6 the previous year.

But the Dartmouth head coach had prepared his team well for Cornell. He had planned some special defensive formations just for the Cornell game.

The new Dartmouth formations worked. The Big Red offense that had averaged more than 30 points a game sputtered in the first half. The score was tied 0–0 when the teams headed to their locker rooms at halftime. Still, the Cornell team wasn't worried. As the Cornell captain and quarterback Walter Matuszak recalled many years later for an article in the *Boston Globe*, "Everyone thought we had a real fine chance of winning."

But Cornell continued to struggle in the second half. The late autumn afternoon in New Hampshire grew darker and colder.

Early in the fourth quarter, Dartmouth kicked a 27-yard field goal to take a surprising 3–0 lead.

By then, snow had begun to swirl in the air. Cornell and its eighteen-game unbeaten streak—and its number one ranking—were in real trouble.

Finally, late in the game, Cornell forced Dartmouth to punt. The Big Red got the ball on its own 48-yard line with only a minute and 30 seconds left on the clock. Two quick passes and a defensive pass interference call against Dartmouth moved the ball to Dartmouth's 17-yard line. Mort Landsberg, the Cornell fullback, blasted through the Dartmouth defense to the six-yard line and a first down.

With less than a minute remaining and time running out, the Dartmouth defense held on. Three Cornell running plays moved the ball down to the one-yard line. After a penalty against Cornell moved the ball back to the six-yard line, Cornell tried a pass into the end zone that the Dartmouth defense swatted away.

With two seconds left on the scoreboard clock and the snow falling harder, confusion reigned on the field. Some Dartmouth players and even one official thought it should be Dartmouth's ball because Cornell had not scored in the regulation four downs. But the head referee pointed to the official scoreboard in Dartmouth's Memorial Stadium (there were no sideline down markers in 1940). The officials running the scoreboard in the snow and the confusion surrounding the final Cornell drive had missed a play. The scoreboard mistakenly indicated that it was fourth down. Cornell had one more chance to score.

Thinking that it truly was fourth down, Cornell decided not to kick a tying field goal and instead threw a touchdown pass. Cornell had won—or seemed to have won— by a score of 7–3.

Following the game, some Dartmouth players and fans insisted that Cornell had won the game on a mistaken fifth down. But the game was in the books as a 7–3 Cornell victory, and no rule allowed Dartmouth to change it.

The next afternoon, Coach Snavely reviewed the game films and saw the officials' mistake. He called in his players and showed them the final minute. "We must have looked at that film a hundred times. There was no doubt about it," team captain Matuszak recalled. Cornell had scored the winning touchdown on a fifth down.

Coach Snavely left the decision of what to do to his players. The Cornell team elected to give Dartmouth a 3–0 victory. "I think the vote was near unanimous," Matuszak remembered.

The next day, Cornell athletic director James Lynah and Coach Carl Snavely sent a telegram to the Dartmouth athletic director that read, "In view of the conclusions reached by the officials that the Cornell touchdown was scored on a fifth down, Cornell relinquishes claim to the victory and extends congratulations to Dartmouth." The Dartmouth athletic director wired back, "Dartmouth accepts the victory and your congratulations and salutes the Cornell team."

With the exchange of telegrams, Cornell's

unbeaten streak and its chance for a national championship were gone.

The Cornell players' decision, like the decision made by Sam and the Cowboys, was not an easy one. The game was over and Cornell had officially won. No rule required the Cornell players to give the victory to Dartmouth. According to the Cornell University website, the 1940 Cornell-Dartmouth football game remains the only time a college sporting event has been decided after the completion of the game.

Fifty years later the University of Colorado football team was presented with a similar situation. Because of a referee's mistake, Colorado scored a touchdown on a fifth down to beat Missouri 33–31 on the final play of the game. When shown evidence of the referee's mistake, the Colorado coaches and team decided to keep the victory.

By giving the win to Dartmouth, the Cornell players showed they were true champions. And, as Sam's father said, the good sportsmanship of the Cornell players is still remembered. "As the years went on, nobody remembered the undefeated season," Matuszak said. "They [remembered] the fifth down."

Acknowledgments

Much of the information about the 1940 game between Cornell and Dartmouth came from the article "Men of Honor" by Bob Duffy, published in the *Boston Globe* on December 29, 2001.

The author also wishes to thank Steve Willertz, longtime coach of the Severn Seminoles in Anne Arundel County, Maryland, for his help with the diagrams of the football plays and for his lessons in football terminology.

About the Author

Fred Bowen was a Little Leaguer who loved to read. Now he is the author of many action-packed books of sports fiction. He has also written a weekly sports column for kids in the *Washington Post* since 2000.

For thirteen years, Fred coached kids' baseball and basketball teams. Some of his stories spring directly from his coaching experience and his sports-happy childhood in Marblehead, Massachusetts.

Fred holds a degree in history from the University of Pennsylvania and a law degree from George Washington University. He was a lawyer for many years before retiring to become a full-time children's author. Bowen has been a guest author at schools and conferences across the country, as well as the Smithsonian Institute in Washington, D.C., and The Baseball Hall of Fame.

Fred lives in Silver Spring, Maryland, with his wife Peggy Jackson. Their son is a college baseball coach and their daughter is a college student.

For more information
check out the author's website at
www.fredbowen.com.

Hey, sports fans!

Don't miss all the action-packed books by Fred Bowen.
Check out www.SportsStorySeries.com for more info.

Fred Bowen Sports Story Series

All-St★r Sports Story
Series

T. J.'s Secret Pitch
PB: $5.95 / 978-1-56145-504-1 / 1-56145-504-0

T. J.'s pitches just don't pack the power they need to strike out the batters, but the story of 1940s baseball hero Rip Sewell and his legendary eephus pitch may help him find a solution.

The Golden Glove
PB: $5.95 / 978-1-56145-505-8 / 1-56145-505-9

Without his lucky glove, Jamie doesn't believe in his ability to lead his baseball team to victory. How will he learn that faith in oneself is the most important equipment for any game?

The Kid Coach
PB: $5.95 / 978-1-56145-506-5 / 1-56145-506-7

Scott and his teammates can't find an adult to coach their team, so they must find a leader among themselves.

Playoff Dreams
PB: $5.95 / 978-1-56145-507-2 / 1-56145-507-5

Brendan is one of the best players in the league, but no matter how hard he tries, he can't make his team win.

Winners Take All
PB: $5.95 / 978-1-56145-512-6 / 1-56145-512-1

Kyle makes a poor decision to cheat in a big game. Someone discovers the truth and threatens to reveal it. What can Kyle do now?

Want more?

All-Star Sports Story Series

Full Court Fever
PB: $5.95 / 978-1-56145-508-9 / 1-56145-508-3

The Falcons have the skill but not the height to win their games. Will the full-court zone press be the solution to their problem?

Off the Rim
PB: $5.95 / 978-1-56145-509-6 / 1-56145-509-1

Hoping to be more than a benchwarmer, Chris learns that defense is just as important as offense.

The Final Cut
PB: $5.95 / 978-1-56145-510-2 / 1-56145-510-5

Four friends realize that they may not all make the team and that the tryouts are a test—not only of their athletic skills, but of their friendship as well.

On the Line
PB: $5.95 / 978-1-56145-511-9 / 1-56145-511-3

Marcus is the highest scorer and the best rebounder, but he's not so great at free throws—until the school custodian helps him overcome his fear of failure.